the CRiTTER club

Liz Learns a Lesson

by Callie Barkley 🐾 illustrated by Marsha Riti

LITTLE SIMON

New York London Toronto Sydney New Delhi

LITTLE SIMON

An imprint of Simon & Schuster Children's Publishing Division 1230 Avenue of the Americas, New York, New York 10020 Copyright © 2013 by Simon & Schuster, Inc. All rights reserved, including the right of reproduction in whole or in part in any form. LITTLE SIMON is a registered trademark of Simon & Schuster, Inc., and associated colophon is a trademark of Simon & Schuster, Inc. For information about special discounts for bulk purchases, please contact Simon & Schuster Special Sales at 1-866-506-1949 or business@simonandschuster.com. The Simon & Schuster Speakers Bureau can bring authors to your live event. For more information or to book an event contact the Simon & Schuster Speakers Bureau at 1-866-248-3049 or visit our website at www.simonspeakers.com. Designed by Laura Roode.

Manufactured in the United States of America 0413 FFG

First Edition 10 9 8 7 6 5 4 3 2 1

Library of Congress Cataloging-in-Publication Data Barkley, Callie. Liz learns a lesson / by Callie Barkley ; illustrated by Marsha Riti. — 1st ed. p. cm. — (The Critter Club ; #3) Summary: Members of the Critter Club are all excited about their summer plans until Liz learns that, instead of taking an art class, she will have to be in summer school to improve her math skills, but a fun teacher, a classroom pet, support from her friends, and advice from her brother might get her through. [etc.] [1. Schools—Fiction. 2. Mathematics—Fiction. 3. Friendship—Fiction. 4. Clubs—Fiction. 5. Animal shelters—Fiction.] I. Riti, Marsha, ill. II. Title. PZ7.B250585Li 2013 [Fic]—dc23 2012018750

ISBN 978-1-4424-6768-2 (pbk)

ISBN 978-1-4424-6770-5 (hc)

ISBN 978-1-4424-6771-2 (eBook)

Table of Contents

Chapter 1

Hello, Summer!

Liz sat down on the bright green grass. She closed her eyes and soaked up the late-afternoon sunshine. "Can you believe it?" she said to her friends Ellie, Amy, and Marion. "Tomorrow is the *last day of school*!"

"Hel-lo, summer!" Ellie cried joyfully. "Hello, ice cream and

swimming and flip-flops—"

"And hello, lots of Critter Club!" added Amy.

The Critter Club was an animal rescue shelter the girls helped start.

Their friend Ms. Sullivan had come up with the idea after the girls found her lost puppy, Rufus. Amy's mom, a veterinarian, was a huge help too. Together they had turned Ms. Sullivan's big, empty barn into a cozy shelter for lost and lonely animals.

Thanks to The Critter Club, three abandoned bunnies had new homes. Right now the club had no animal guests . . . except for Rufus, of course!

That was about to change.

Marion opened her notebook.

Critter Club Pet Sitting

Family	Pet	Name
Perez	Cat	Lentils
Hall	Dog	Ewok
Walker	3 Rabbits	Floppy, Flippy, + Steve
	Dog	Duke
Stein	Guinea Pig	Jose
Reed	Cat	Dax
Gray	Cat	Dr. Claw
Brooks	Dog	Spencer
Bruni	2 mice	Mac + Izzy
Gonzalez	Dog	Tootsie
Adams		

"We've already got ten families signed up for pet sitting!" she said.

Ellie let out a happy squeal. "Yay! Amy's mom was right. Pet sitting was such a great idea!"

"I think so too," said Amy. "While families are away on summer vacation, their pets can stay here!"

Liz flopped backward onto the soft, warm grass. She was *so* happy and excited. She'd get to spend lots of time with her friends, *and* she was done with homework until September!

Liz didn't mind school, but she sometimes had a hard time with school*work*—especially math. She would definitely not miss math over vacation.

The girls talked about their other summer plans. Marion was going to music day camp in July. She had been taking piano lessons since she was five.

Amy was going to help out at her mom's vet clinic. She also planned to spend a lot of weekends with her

dad in Orange Blossom. "He just got a new pool in his backyard!" Amy explained.

Ellie and her little brother, Toby, had fun plans with their grand-mother, Nana Gloria. "She's going to take us to the roller rink and the

zoo and the Santa Vista pool!" Ellie
said excitedly.

Liz sat up on the grass. "Well,
guess what I'm doing?" she said.

"Art?" asked Ellie, Marion, and
Amy at the same time. All four girls
started laughing.

"How did you guess?" Liz said

with a grin. Of course, her
friends knew she loved to paint and
draw. Mrs. Cummings's art room
was Liz's favorite place at school.
There, she never felt like the one
who didn't "get it"—unlike when

she was in math class.

"Okay, you're right!" Liz said. "Mrs. Cummings is teaching a class in June at the Santa Vista Library!" Liz glanced at Amy. "I'll look for you there?"

Amy giggled and nodded. "In the mystery section. I plan to read every Nancy Drew they've got. But first, I will see you all at school tomorrow . . . for our last day!"

The girls hopped onto their bikes and headed to their homes for dinner.

Liz took a deep, happy breath

as she pedaled. The warm air blew through her wavy blond hair.

Just one more day of school, she thought. *Then, let the summer begin!*

Change of Plans

The last day of school is so fun! thought Liz.

She was on the playground, trying not to get tagged. Their teacher, Mrs. Sienna, had taken the class outside for an extra recess. Earlier, in their classroom, they had played Simon Says. Even the teachers were in the mood to have fun.

Back inside, Mrs. Sienna found a note on her desk. "Liz Jenkins," she said, "Mrs. Young would like to see you." Mrs. Young was the school principal.

"Me?" said Liz. "Oh . . . okay." She turned and headed for the main office. She felt a nervous flutter in her stomach. Had she done

something wrong? But Liz pushed
the worry out of her mind. After all,
what could go wrong on the last
day of school?

Minutes later she was stand-
ing in the doorway of Mrs. Young's
office.

"Hi, Liz," Mrs. Young said kindly.

Someone else was there too, with her back to Liz. She turned.

"Mom!" Liz sighed with relief. "Did I forget my lunch again?"

Mrs. Jenkins smiled at Liz. "No, honey," she said. "That's not why I'm here. Come have a seat." Her mom tapped the seat of the chair

next to her. "Mrs. Young and I were just talking about math."

She handed Liz a yellow piece of paper.

MATH SUMMER SCHOOL!

Sharpen your skills over the summer.

When: Weekdays in June, 9:00 a.m. to noon

Where: Santa Vista Elementary School library

MATH? thought Liz. *In the summer?!* That sounded awful. Who would want to do *that*?

"Liz," said her mom, "we know you've had a hard time with math this year—even though you've tried your best. This class will give you a little extra help."

"But Mom," said Liz, "what about my art class?" She pointed to the flyer. "Both classes meet at the same time."

"I'm afraid you *need* to take this math class," Mrs. Young said. "You need it to keep up with the rest of the students."

Liz's mom put her arm around Liz. "I'm sorry, honey, but you're going to have to miss the art class with Mrs. Cummings."

Liz felt tears welling up in her eyes. Across the desk Mrs. Young suddenly looked blurry.

"The good news is that the math teacher, Mr. Brown, is very nice and funny," Mrs. Young said. "You'll have a blast. How does that sound?"

It sounded to Liz like she had no choice.

It sounded like the start of the worst summer ever.

chapter 3

Liz's Secret

Liz tried to enjoy the rest of the day. It was hard. She couldn't stop thinking about summer school.

After school Ellie invited Liz, Amy, and Marion over to her house, but Liz just felt like going home. She wasn't ready to share her bad news. She felt so embarrassed.

I must just be the worst math

student in the whole grade, Liz thought to herself.

Liz told Ellie she wasn't feeling very well. "Oh, you poor thing," Ellie said. "You have to get better soon! After all it's the summer! There are so many things to do! And we have lots of plans!"

At home Liz's mom was waiting for her. She had made a batch of Liz's favorite organic cookies.

They sat down together at the

kitchen table, and Liz took a cookie. They talked more about summer school. "It probably won't help." Liz moped. "I just don't get math."

Her mom smiled. "When I was in college, there was this beautiful oak tree in the town park. After a storm it lost some big branches. The

town was going to cut it down. They said it was old and sick and too dangerous to have in the park."

Liz nodded and reached for another cookie. "So what happened?"

"Well, some friends and I called a tree specialist. We found out the tree *could* be healthy again with some special care. So we started a petition, and we got thousands of people to sign it," her mom said. "And guess what?"

"You saved the tree?" Liz guessed.

"We saved the tree!" her mom exclaimed, jumping out of her seat. Liz giggled. She loved how excited her mom got about nature.

Mrs. Jenkins sat down again. "Do you know why I told you that story, Liz?"

Liz pretended to think about it. "Does it have to do with math?"

Her mom nodded. "At first saving the tree seemed impossible. But each day we took tiny steps toward our goal—and we got there."

Liz felt better after talking to her mom. Dinner helped too. When her dad and her brother, Stewart, got home, her mom fired up the grill. Tofu dogs were, by far, Liz's

favorite summertime food.

After dinner Ellie stopped by. "I can't stay long," she told Liz. "I just wanted to see how you're feeling."

Liz smiled, thinking what a good friend Ellie was. "Actually, I *am* feeling better," she said.

She and Ellie sat down on the front steps. Liz told her about

summer school. "I was really upset about it before. That's what I meant about not feeling well."

Ellie linked arms with Liz. "Aw, I'm sorry, Liz," she said. "I know how excited you were about the class with Mrs. Cummings."

They sat for a minute, side by side, without saying anything. Crickets chirped loudly all around them.

"Look at it this way," Ellie said. "You still have afternoons at The Critter Club. And you'll have all of July and August when you're done!"

"That's true," said Liz with a

nod. "I will have that." She squeezed Ellie's arm. "And I will have a great friend like you, too."

Pop Quiz!

Monday came too soon for Liz. It was the first day of summer school. At 8:55 a.m. she and her mom walked into the school lobby. It was strangely quiet.

Grrrrr, Liz grumbled silently. It felt like the *whole world* was on summer vacation. Her brother, Stewart, was still in bed!

In the library Liz's mom signed her in and they met Mr. Brown. He seemed nice enough to Liz, but she was distracted. She looked around the room. Was there anyone else here she knew?

There were about ten other kids, but Liz saw no familiar faces. *It's bad enough that I stink at math,* she thought. *Now all these other kids are going to find that out, too!*

Liz's mom said good-bye. "I'll

pick you up at noon," she told Liz.
"Remember, day by day. Tiny steps."

Liz took an empty seat at a table.
She shot a quick smile at the boy
and girl already sitting there. They
smiled back.

"Okay, everybody," Mr. Brown said. "Welcome to 'Melting Math.'" He laughed. "Get it? It's summertime? And math is cool? So the math is melting?"

Liz knew Mr. Brown was just trying to get everyone in a good mood, but she was still feeling grumpy. No one else laughed either.

"Never mind that," Mr. Brown continued cheerfully. "First things first." He passed out a sheet of paper to each of them. "Pop quiz!"

The class groaned.

What?! thought Liz. *A quiz? Already?*

Then Liz looked down at the quiz.

1) What is your name?

2) What is your favorite color?

3) What is your favorite ice-cream flavor?

4) If you weren't here, where would you be?

Okay, thought Liz. *Mr. Brown might be kind of fun, after all.*

After the quiz Mr. Brown passed out math problems. "Work with the others at your table," he said. "Then we'll go over the answers together."

Liz smiled again at the kids she was sitting with. "Hi," she said. "I'm

Liz. You guys don't go to school here, do you?"

The boy shook his head. "No," he said. "I go to Orange Blossom Elementary. My name is Robert." He smiled shyly.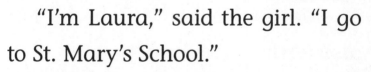

"I'm Laura," said the girl. "I go to St. Mary's School."

They figured out that they were all the same age—eight! They also figured out that they would *all* rather be doing something else.

When Laura looked down at the worksheet, she frowned. "Oh no. Greater than, less than. I cannot keep those straight to save my life."

"Me neither," said Robert. "I'm also terrible at subtraction."

Liz smiled. Here were other kids with math struggles—just like her. She felt herself start to relax.

"And fractions!" Liz added.

"What is with fractions? How can three-eighths be *less* than one-half? Three is more than one and eight is more than two!"

Robert and Laura laughed at Liz's joke—not at Liz. Liz knew right then that the three of them were going to be friends.

The Critter Club

Book your summer
pet sitting now.

Critter Sitters

Liz told her mom all about class on the drive home. She could hardly wait to tell her friends, too.

At home Liz grabbed a sandwich before she hopped on her bike and headed for The Critter Club. Ellie, Amy, and Marion were all there organizing pet food and supplies.

When they saw Liz, they came

over and gave her a big group hug. "I guess everyone knows?" Liz asked. She looked at Ellie.

"I hope you don't mind!" Ellie said. "The girls were worried—wondering where you were."

Liz smiled. "I don't mind."

"Oh, okay," said Ellie. "Then tell us all about it! Don't leave anything out!"

"Ellie, give her a break," Amy teased her friend.

"No, it's okay," Liz said. "I was nervous this morning, but it wasn't so bad."

The girls sat down in a circle, each on an upside-down bucket.

"Is school really empty and quiet?" Ellie wanted to know.

"Do you know anyone in class?" Amy asked.

"And what's the teacher like?" Marion questioned.

Liz told them all about it—about Mr. Brown, the fun pop quiz, and Robert and Laura. "There's going to be a test every Friday." Liz looked around the barn. "So what did I miss?" she asked her friends.

Ellie, Amy, and Marion looked at each other. They shared a secret

smile. "Should we show her now?" Ellie asked.

"What?" asked Liz. "Show me what?"

They led her over to a glass tank on a side table. "The Kim family dropped off their pet this morning,"

said Amy. "They're going on a four-week cruise. So we're going to watch Herman."

"Um, no," said Ellie. "*Liz* is going to watch Herman. *I* am not watching Herman."

Liz looked in the tank. Sitting on one of the rocks was a big fuzzy tarantula!

"He is so adorable!" cooed Liz. She put her face close to the glass. "Hi, Herman!"

Of all the girls Liz was the one most into . . . *unusual* pets. She had a pet ferret named Reggie, whom she adored. As Liz liked to say, all pets needed love: mice, salamanders, snakes, Madagascar hissing cockroaches. . . .

Liz grinned through the glass at the spider. "Herman," she said. "This summer is looking up!"

An Extra Student

The next morning Liz rode her bike to school. Laura was at the bike rack.

"Hi, Liz!" Laura said as she parked her own bike.

"Hi, Laura!" Liz replied. "You live close enough to bike too?"

Laura nodded. "Yep. I live about three blocks away. Over by the public library."

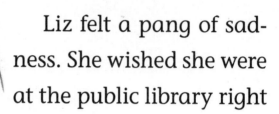

Liz felt a pang of sadness. She wished she were at the public library right now, at Mrs. Cummings's art class, instead of in her school's library.

Just then a car pulled up in the drop-off circle. Robert hopped out.

"Hi!" he said, walking over to Liz and Laura. "What did you guys think of the homework?"

Liz groaned. "Ugh!" she said. The three of them headed for the school entrance. "Regrouping is another thing I'm terrible at."

"Me too," said Robert.

"Me three," said Laura. Suddenly she stopped in her tracks. "Hey, that's a crazy-looking rock," she said, pointing at the ground.

Liz and Robert stopped too. There was a brownish green rock right on the sidewalk. It had some kind of pattern on it. "Oh, wow," said Robert. "*Is* it a rock? Or is it a . . . ?"

Slowly, a little head peeked out from under the rock. Then four little legs appeared. The rock started to move!

"It's a turtle!" Liz exclaimed happily. "Cool!"

Moving carefully, the three of them knelt by the turtle's side. "He's so beautiful," Liz said.

"Where do you think he came from?" Robert asked.

Liz looked around. "I think there's a little pond back there," she said. She pointed toward the woods next to the school. "Maybe he lives there."

"Maybe he's someone's pet?" Laura suggested.

They stood watching the turtle walk in slow motion. He was inching— very, very slowly— toward the street.

"I don't think we should leave

him here," Liz said. "What if he crawls into the road?"

They had to get to class. Liz made a quick decision. She emptied her backpack. She gently picked up the turtle and placed him carefully at the bottom. Then she zipped the bag back up, but not all the way.

"Come on," she said, picking up her homework sheets. "Let's get to class!"

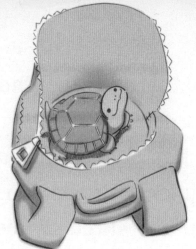

Robert and Laura looked at each other, their eyes wide. Robert shrugged. Laura giggled. Liz smiled, a twinkle in her eye.

Then, together, they hurried to class.

Mr. Brown began class by writing some addition problems on the whiteboard.

Under the table Liz's backpack wiggled. *I hope he has enough air in there*, Liz thought.

"Okay!" Mr. Brown said. "So, for which problems will you need to regroup?" He called on a girl at another table.

While she answered, Liz peeked under the table.

Is it too dry for him in there?, Liz wondered.

"Great!" Mr. Brown was saying to the girl. "Who else? Are there any other problems here that will need regrouping?" He called on Robert.

Maybe I should take the turtle to the bathroom, Liz thought. *He could swim in the sink.*

"Good, Robert," Mr. Brown said.

"Now there's just one left. One more problem on the board that will need regrouping. Who can tell me which . . . ?"

What if he's hungry? Liz was thinking. *But what do turtles eat, anyway?*

"Liz?" Mr. Brown called. "Liz, can you tell me?"

Startled, Liz jumped a little in her seat. "Oh! Uh . . ." She hadn't heard the question. What should she say? She shifted in her seat. Her right leg bumped

her backpack under the table. It fell over.

Liz squealed loudly, then blurted out: *"Turtle!"*

She reached down and propped the backpack up. When she sat up again, everyone was staring at her.

Liz flashed a smile. She tried to act natural, but she could feel her cheeks blush.

"Liz, do you have something to share with the class?" Mr. Brown asked.

She looked across the table at Robert and Laura. They were both trying to contain their laughter.

Then Liz picked up her backpack and stood up. She walked over to Mr. Brown's desk. She reached inside her backpack and pulled out the turtle.

The whole class gasped, and the turtle slowly pulled its head into its shell.

What would Mr. Brown say?

"See, he was outside on the sidewalk," Liz explained. "It looked like he was headed into the street. I didn't want to leave him. . . ."

Mr. Brown's eyes were wide. He looked surprised, but was he mad? For a moment Liz couldn't tell . . . until his mouth turned up at the corners. He was smiling! Then he was laughing!

"Well, this is a first," he said. "I've never had a reptile in class before!"

Chapter 7

Counting Digits

Liz breathed a sigh of relief. She was glad she wasn't in trouble.

"I bet we can find him a cozier spot," Mr. Brown said. He spotted the librarian's empty fish tank. He let Laura and some others go outside to find some rocks. Meanwhile, Mr. Brown took Liz and Robert with him to get water.

"Make it *warm* water," Robert told Mr. Brown. "My dad once had a turtle and they like it warm."

"Oh! And I can find out what turtles like to eat," said Liz. "I'll bring food for him tomorrow."

Before long, the tank was the perfect turtle home.

"Our new friend looks very happy," said Mr. Brown.

"Now let's get back to math."

"*Awww!*" everyone moaned.

But Mr. Brown had some fun up his sleeve. "We're going to use math to name our turtle friend."

"Hooray!" the class cheered.

Mr. Brown laughed. "See? Math

can be fun!" Together they made a list of some math-themed names. Mr. Brown wrote them all on the whiteboard.

Then the class voted. Each person put a tally mark next to their favorite.

"Well, it looks like our turtle

has a name," said Mr. Brown. "Welcome, Digit!"

• • • ◌ • • • • • • • • • • • ♥ • • • •

As the first week of class went on, everyone seemed excited to have a class pet—even Mr. Brown.

On Wednesday they worked on greater than and less than. Liz's favorite problem was:

Which is greater :
a million turtles or
a billion turtles?

On Thursday they did word problems. Some were really tricky.

Digit crawls two inches on Sunday, ten inches on Monday, and twelve inches on Tuesday. How many feet does Digit crawl all together?

Liz added the numbers: 2 + 10 + 12. She wrote down her answer: twenty-four. She raised her hand.

"Before I call on anyone, here's a hint," said Mr. Brown. "The first step in solving a word problem is not getting the *answer*. It's getting the *question*."

Huh? thought Liz. She reread the problem. This time she noticed: How many *feet* does Digit crawl all

together? She erased her 24. Twenty-four inches was the same as . . .

Mr. Brown called on her. "Two feet!" Liz said.

"Excellent, Liz!" Mr. Brown said.

Finally it was Friday—test day. Mr. Brown went over everything they had covered that week. Then he passed out the test papers.

Liz took a deep breath. She had stayed home from The Critter Club on Thursday afternoon so she could study hard. She'd asked Ellie to tell Amy and Marion why. Then, after dinner that evening, Ellie had called on the phone. "Everybody says, 'Good luck!' You're going to do great!"

Liz picked up her pencil. "I hope Ellie's right," she whispered to herself.

The library was silent for the rest of the class. Liz worked hard and lost track of time.

After class Liz walked out into the sunshine. Laura was right behind her. "So, what did you think?" she asked Liz.

"You know," said Liz, "it wasn't *too* bad."

Actually, for the first time ever, Liz felt like she wasn't totally awful at math.

Chapter 8

Day by Day

The weeks started to fly by. In the mornings Liz went to class. She saw Laura and Robert. She checked on Digit. She tried hard in math, and it was paying off! On her first three tests, Liz got most of the questions right!

Every day, after stopping home for lunch, she went to The Critter

Club. Sometimes all four of the girls were there. Other times it was just two or three of them. Their June schedule was hanging in the barn.

JUNE

Sun	Mon	Tue	Wed	Thu	Fri	Sat
						1 Marion Horse Show
2	3 Ellie w/ Nana Gloria Marion Piano Lesson	4 Amy working at vet clinic	5 Marion Piano Lesson	6 Amy working at vet clinic	7 Ellie w/ Nana Gloria	8
9 Amy day at Dad's	10 Marion Piano Lesson	11 Amy working at vet clinic	12 Ellie w/ Nana Gloria Marion Piano Lesson	13 Amy working at vet clinic	14 Ellie w/ Nana Gloria	15
16 Ellie w/ Nana Gloria	17 Marion Piano Lesson	18 Ellie w/ Nana Gloria Amy working at vet clinic	19 Marion Piano Lesson	20 Amy working at vet clinic	21	22 Marion Horse Show
23 Amy day at Dad's	24 Marion Piano Lesson	25 Amy working at vet clinic	26 Marion Piano Lesson	27 Amy working at vet clinic	28 Ellie w/ Nana Gloria	29
30						

Of course Liz had told Robert and Laura all about The Critter Club. On a few afternoons they came to help out too. They both loved animals. Plus, it was great to have the extra help. For part of

June the club was superbusy. They were pet sitting for four dogs, three cats, some mice, a guinea pig, three rabbits—and Herman the tarantula. It took a lot of work to keep them all happy!

At dinnertime Liz rode her bike home. Her route took her right past the Santa Vista Library. Liz still felt sad about missing her art class, but she just tried not to think about it too much.

Day after day, week after week, Liz worked hard.

On the last Wednesday evening in June, Liz was in her room. She was working on a homework sheet when she suddenly realized something.

The last test is . . . tomorrow!

It had slipped Liz's mind until now. Usually *Friday* was test day, but this was the final week of class. Mr. Brown had said that their test would be on *Thursday.* He would hand them back on Friday, the last day of class!

Liz felt a little panicked. *Can I*

do it? she wondered. *What if I completely mess this one up?* She dug around in her backpack for her practice sheets. "I have to go over everything from this week!" she told her ferret, Reggie.

Just then Liz's brother, Stewart, popped into her room. Stewart was twelve years old. The two of them got along okay, but lately Stewart had been teasing her about math.

He thought he was so smart, just because he was in sixth grade.

"Hey, Lizzie," he said.

"Not now, Stewart!" Liz snapped at him. "I don't have time to be made fun of! Tomorrow's my last math test."

"Who? *Me?*" Stewart said. "I wasn't going to tease you."

Liz squinted at him. Was he telling the truth?

"Hey, how's that turtle you found?" Stewart asked.

"Digit?" said Liz. "He's good. He's eating a lot!"

Stewart nodded. "Well, I think it's cool that you saved him. Turtles

are awesome! They just do their own thing. They can't be rushed. 'Slow and steady wins the race,' and all that." Stewart turned to go, then stopped. "Hey, that's a good tip for the test, right?"

Liz watched Stewart go. Her brother sometimes said crazy stuff. *But this time*, thought Liz, *he kind of makes sense.*

The next morning Liz got to school a few minutes early. She was ready to go!

She stopped by Digit's tank.

"Don't tell Stewart," she whispered, "but I'm going to take his advice. Slow and steady wins the race. Right, Digit?"

Robert came in, then Laura. They both gave Liz a thumbs-up.

Mr. Brown spent most of the class doing a big review. Then he passed out the test papers.

Liz took a deep breath. *Stay calm,* she told herself. *Don't rush. Check your work. You'll be fine.* Liz picked up her pencil, and she began.

For the rest of the class the only sound came from pencils scratching on papers. Liz finished just as Mr. Brown stood up. "Pencils down," he said. He collected the papers. "See you all tomorrow! I'll pass back your graded tests then."

Liz could hardly wait until tomorrow's class!

Chapter 9

The Final Grade

Liz had that fluttery feeling in her stomach again. It was the last day of summer school, and Mr. Brown was about to pass back the tests.

Liz could hardly sit still. She couldn't stand not knowing how she'd done! She had been thinking about it since she finished the test the day before. At The Critter Club

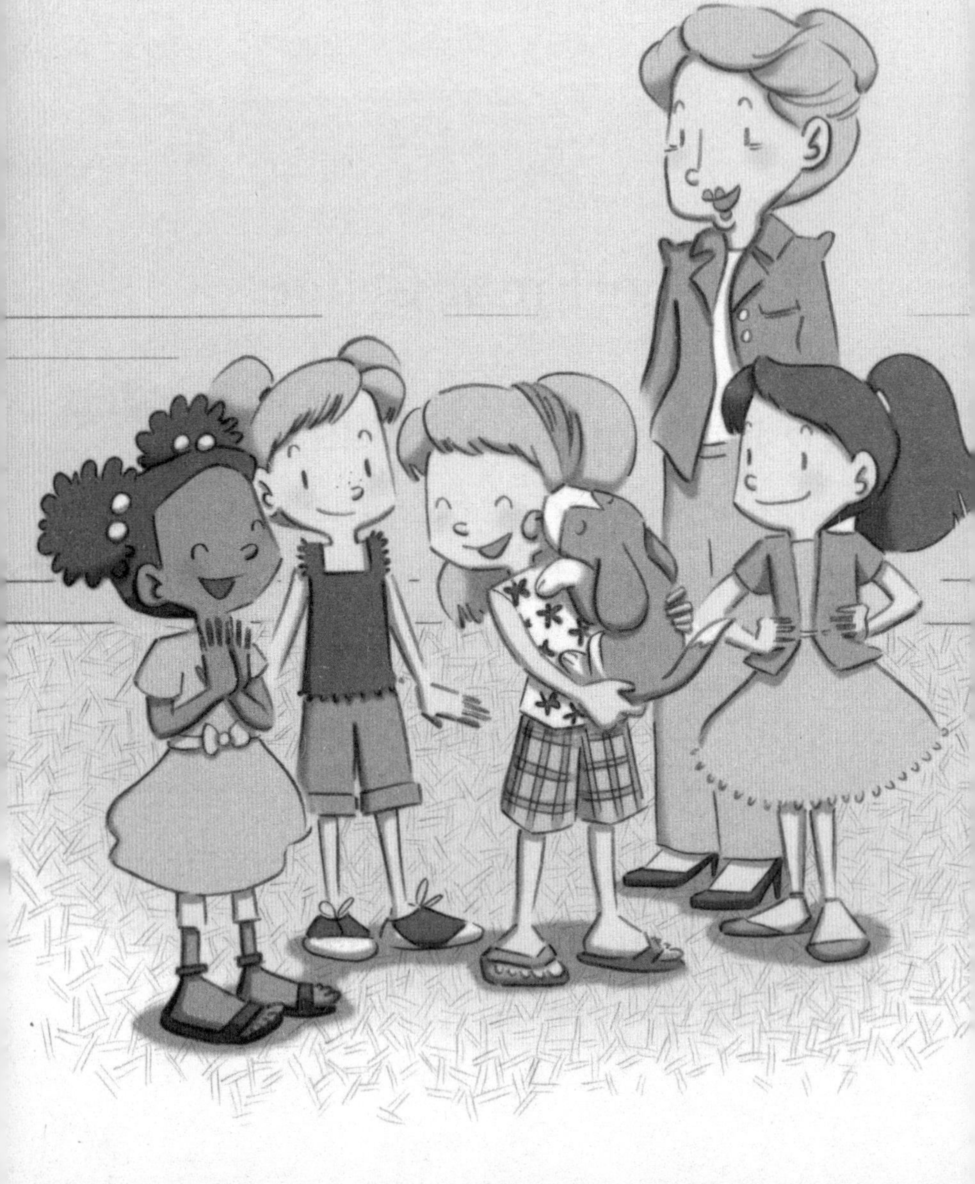

afterward, her friends had been so happy for her.

"You've worked really hard and done your best," Marion had said.

Even Ms. Sullivan and Rufus had dropped by the barn. "I'm very proud of you, Liz," Ms. Sullivan said. Rufus jumped up on Liz and licked her cheek.

"Rufus is proud of you too!" Amy joked.

Now, sitting in the library, Liz wondered: What would she tell them if she *hadn't* passed?

"Okay!" said Mr. Brown. "Before

I return the tests, I just want to say something. . . ."

Liz's palms were sweating. She couldn't wait another moment!

"I am so proud of this class," Mr. Brown went on. "You worked very, very hard all month long."

He gave a huge smile. "Oh! And there's one more thing . . . you all passed! Congratulations!"

"Hooray!" the class cheered. Liz jumped up out of her seat. Laura and Robert jumped up too.

"Great job, Liz," Mr. Brown said. He held out her test. She took it and

looked at the grade at the top. It was an A!

I got an A? she thought. *In MATH?* "Yahoo!" Liz cried. She could not wait to show her mom and dad—and Stewart, too!

Robert and Laura also did well! Everyone was so excited!

And just like that summer school was over! Kids gathered their things and headed for the door. Laura and Robert got up to leave.

"Hey," said Liz, "maybe we could meet up later at The Critter Club?"

"I'll ask my mom!" Laura said.

"Me too!" said Robert. "Gotta run. My mom's going to flip when she sees my test!"

Laura and Robert headed out, but Liz hung back. She walked up to Mr. Brown. "Good-bye, Mr. Brown," she said. "And thanks a lot. You know, you actually made math pretty fun."

"Thanks, Liz!" Mr. Brown said. "And you know what else? You're much better at math than you think you are."

Liz beamed. *"Really?"* she said.

Mr. Brown nodded. "Yep! It's okay if it takes you longer than others. It doesn't mean you can't get there." He looked over at Digit's tank. "Right, Digit?"

Then he said, "Oh! Speaking of Digit . . . I'm going on vacation in a few days. Do you think Digit could go home with you? Would your parents mind?"

A smile spread across Liz's face. "Don't worry, Mr. Brown," she said. "I know a place where Digit will be well taken care of."

The Critter Club had just gotten one more guest.

The Best Day Ever

At home Liz's mom took one look at her test and gave Liz a big hug. "I am *so* proud of you, honey! This calls for a celebration!"

Liz's mom picked up the phone. She called Robert's parents and Laura's parents. She asked if the kids could come out for lunch.

An hour later Liz and her

mom picked them both up. The four of them went to Liz's favorite restaurant.

Digit came along too. Liz gave him some turtle food pellets so they could all eat together.

After lunch Liz's mom dropped

them off at The Critter Club. They were excited to show Digit around.

Laura and Robert hopped out of the car. As Liz carried Digit's tank out, she said, "Thanks, Mom! See you later at home."

"Oh, Liz! Wait!" her mom called. "I was so excited about your test, I almost forgot to tell you!"

"Tell me what?" Liz asked.

"I saw Mrs. Cummings at the grocery store," Liz's mom said. "She's teaching another art class at the library in July. How does that sound?" Her mom was smiling.

Liz's mouth fell open. She had to put Digit down. She didn't want to drop him while she jumped up and down for joy!

Liz threw her head back and shouted, "This *is* going to be the best summer after all!"

Read on for a sneak peek at
the next Critter Club book:

#4

Marion Takes a Break

In the school cafeteria Marion saw Amy, Ellie, and Liz sitting near the window. Marion hurried over. She hoped she would have time to eat her lunch. The recess bell was going to ring in just ten minutes!

"What took you so long?" Amy asked. She scooted down the bench to make space for Marion.

"I couldn't find my lunch!" Marion said, sitting down. "I thought it was in my cubby, but it was in my backpack under my ballet shoes and my leotard."

I've got to get organized! Marion thought as she started to eat. *Better add that to my to-do list!*

Marion was good at making lists. It helped to keep her busy life in order. Now that it was fall, Marion was busier than ever! She worked very hard in school and always got perfect grades. She also had piano lessons and ballet class every week.

Then there was her horse, Coco. Marion went to the stables at least three times a week. Having a horse was a lot of work, but Marion loved every bit of it.

"So what were you talking about?" Marion asked. She took a big bite of her sandwich.

"The kittens!" Ellie exclaimed. There was a new litter of kittens at The Critter Club, the animal shelter that the four girls helped run in their friend Ms. Sullivan's barn. The girls had met Ms. Sullivan when they found her lost puppy, Rufus.

After that, Ms. Sullivan decided the town needed an animal shelter. She had an empty barn; Amy's mom, Dr. Purvis, had a lot of advice to offer since she was a veterinarian; and the *girls* had lots of energy—plus a love of animals.

So The Critter Club began! Since then the girls had helped bunnies and a turtle find homes. They had even offered pet sitting over the summer. Now it was up to them to find homes for an entire litter of kittens!

The girls took turns helping out at The Critter Club after school and on weekends. "Liz and I had such a great time at the club yesterday afternoon," said Ellie. "Those kittens are just so cute!"

"That's the thing! It should be easy to find homes for them," Amy said. "I was thinking . . . what about having a big party at The Critter Club? People could come meet the kittens!"

Marion, Ellie, and Liz all nodded enthusiastically.

"We could have music!" Ellie

The kittens' mother was a stray cat. When a teacher found them all behind the school, she brought them to Dr. Purvis's clinic. Dr. Purvis had suggested that the five healthy kittens stay at The Critter Club, and the girls were very excited to help take care of them!

"The mother cat and one kitten are still at the clinic," Amy told her friends. "Mom says the mama cat needs more rest. And even though the tabby kitten's injured paw is getting better, he still needs to heal a while longer too."

suggested. "I could sing!"

"We could get dressed up!" Marion added. She had a silver dress that would be perfect.

"We could put up pretty lights—and some artwork!" said Liz. She was an amazing artist.

Just then the recess bell rang. Marion chewed fast, trying to fin-ish her sandwich. Then together the four friends headed outside. It was autumn in Santa Vista, but in that part of California, it never got too cold.

Amy walked next to Marion.

"Maybe we'll think of more party ideas this afternoon," Amy said.

"Wait! This afternoon?" Marion mumbled. Her mouth was still full.

"At the Critter Club?" Amy said. "It's Monday—our day to help out. Remember?"

Marion had forgotten! It wasn't like her to get her schedule mixed up.

"Uh, The Critter Club? Of course I will be there!" said Marion, scarfing down the last bite of her lunch.